ROLLO BONES,
Canine Hypnotist

Marshall M. Moyer

TRICYCLE PRESS
Berkeley, California

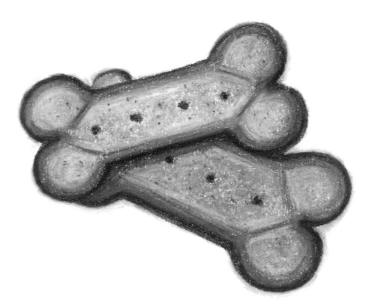

TRICYCLE PRESS
P.O. Box 7123
Berkeley, California 94707

Book design by Marshall M. Moyer and Susan Van Horn
Library of Congress Cataloging-in-Publication Data
Moyer, Marshall M.
Rollo Bones, canine hypnotist / Marshall M. Moyer.
p.   cm.
Summary: Although he has won worldwide success with his ability to hypnotize
human beings, Rollo, a soulful yellow dog, takes a stand for what he really wants to be and do.
ISBN 1-883672-65-1 (hc)
ISBN 1-58246-007-8 (pb)
[1. Dogs—Fiction.   2.Hypnotism—Fiction.]   I. Title.
PZ7.M86664Ro   1998
[E]—dc21
97-44304
CIP
AC
Printed in Singapore
1 2 3 4 5 6 — 03 02 01 00 99 98

Dedicated to my mother, Olive, who read to me as a child.

In memory of Terry and Rob, whose childishness profoundly changed my life.

With special thanks to my chosen family for your support; you know who you are.

Thanks to Mark for always being there to rescue me.

Thanks also to my Duxbury, Massachusetts, Writers Group and to Leon Steinmetz

at the Massachusetts College of Art for your patience, wisdom, and expertise.

And a special dedication to my dalmatian, Barney,

who hypnotizes me on a regular basis.

"Ladies and gentlemen, I am the Amazing Brain, here to entertain you with astounding feats of mind control and powers of suggestion. And I am pleased to present my assistant, Rollo Bones, the Canine Hypnotist!"

Onto the stage ambled Rollo, a yellow dog with soulful eyes. He wagged his tail, and the Brain scratched his ears and whispered, "Good boy."

"May we have a volunteer from the audience?" asked the Brain.

"How about you, madam, with the red hair? Have you ever been hypnotized before?"

"No, I don't really believe in it," she replied, as she stepped up on stage.

"Well, you will. Just relax in this chair."

"Do your stuff," said the Brain, patting Rollo on the head and promising a biscuit.

Rollo sat before the woman and stared intently into her eyes. In seconds, she was deep in a trance. The crowd clapped and whistled. "That's a lovely dress. What wonderful feathers! Now, get up and act like a rooster," the Brain commanded.

The Brain winked at Rollo. Rollo barked once and the woman immediately flew up from the chair.

"Cock-a-doodle-doooo!" she crowed.

The crowd laughed and cheered and stomped its feet. Popcorn sailed through the air. The woman pecked at the kernels.

News of the hypnotizing dog traveled quickly. Every show was a sellout. Rollo became famous and performed before the crowned heads of Europe.

Caught up in their success, the Amazing Brain drove Rollo on and on. Fame and money had gone to his head. Every day got worse: one more drive to one more stage in one more city for one more paycheck. "Hurry up! Let's go! Get your head in the car! Pay attention! Don't make a mess! Stop shedding! Wrong! Don't do that! Do this! Now, listen to me!" said the Brain. "No, no, no!"

Rollo was tired of being treated like some kind of stupid baby. He was the real star, after all. Some peace and quiet was in order.

So the next day at a gas station, Rollo ran away. He rolled in the grass at a nearby park and sniffed everything in sight. He and the Brain used to take lots of walks, he recalled. Now all they did was drive. He remembered other things they used to do together, as he wandered into town.

He passed a store window that was filled with television sets. The Amazing Brain was on every one, holding a poster of Rollo that said, REWARD! "Don't look into his eyes," announced the Brain to the world. "That's how he does it!"

Oh no! thought Rollo. *It's like the TV game shows we used to watch. Now everyone will be looking for me to get the prize money. I have to hide.*

With the help of some clever disguises, Rollo managed to get past the post office,

and the police station,

the fire department,

and the supermarket, without being caught. But he knew it was only a matter of time before he was seen. So he decided to find the Brain and work things out.

Besides, he missed their late-night snacks

and laundry day tugs-of-war,

and, most of all, the hugs and the biscuits.

Rollo hailed a taxi and looked deep into the driver's eyes. "Yes, sir!" said the cabbie. He stepped on the gas.

The taxi screeched away, the tires barely touching the road as they rocketed up to the TV station. At the entrance, the cabbie honked the horn and yelled, "Hey, pal, I got your dog here!" The Amazing Brain rushed to the door with the reward money. The driver took half, slipped the rest to Rollo, and quickly left.

"Bad dog!" yelled the Brain. "Why did you run away?"

Rollo growled and trained his eyes on the Brain's. It was time to teach him a lesson. As Rollo stared, the Amazing Brain began to pant, and sweat trickled down his forehead.

Next, Rollo focused on the TV crew. "Lights! Camera! Action!" they called. "Ladies and gentlemen," the Brain said into the camera, "this is Rollo Bones, the Canine Hypnotist, and I am his assistant, the Amazing Brain. Rollo says, please enjoy our season finale."

Fetch, thought Rollo. *Bring me biscuits and bones.* Off bounded the Brain with a yelp. He quickly returned with the treats.

Now sit! he thought. *Roll over! Now beg. Good Brain, have a biscuit.*

Then Rollo looked deep into the camera. His face filled the TV screen in millions of homes and his big brown eyes let everyone know exactly how he felt.

"Three, two, one . . . and we're off the air," said the studio crew, uncertain of what had happened.

"Why didn't you just tell me you wanted a break?" the Amazing Brain asked Rollo. "I'm willing to compromise. Okay, okay . . . Tell you what: We'll blow off the gig at the Palace and take a vacation."

Rollo wagged his tail and gazed at his partner.

The Brain laughed. "Don't look at me like that, or I'll have to get you dark glasses." Then he hugged Rollo and said, "It's good to have you back."

They walked out to their car and Rollo drove them away.

They noticed people everywhere, out walking and playing with their dogs.
So Rollo parked the car, and he and the Brain joined them for a romp in the grass,
just like the old days.

Now close the book.